Mr Snuffles' Birthday

David Greaves

Illustrated by Emily Wallis

First published 2018 by Clink Street Publishing in association with
Stanage Press Ltd

ISBN: 978-1-912562-31-2 paperback
978-1-912562-32-9 ebook

For the original truffle-snuffler. All my love, always.

It was a wonderful day to be snuffling for truffles;
"What a birthday treat!" thought Mr Snuffles.
But whenever he got to a nice little spot,
Were there truffles to snuffle? There were...NOT!
He looked in the tree stump's mossy hollow;
"No truffles in *there*, to snuffle and swallow."

...And on the wormy woodland floor;
"Not *even one* truffle, to snuffle and gnaw."
...The mossy old log was empty *too*;
"Truffle-less! *Nothing* to snuffle and chew."
Wherever he looked, his truffles were GONE;
There was something fishy going on!

And what he found next was *most* fishy indeed;
In amongst the acorns, roots and seeds –
It was a *half-snuffled* truffle! The rest had been chomped;
The ground all around had *clearly* been stomped!

And from behind the next tree trunk, poking out,
Was a rather long and wrinkly snout
Quivering and hungrily sniffing the breeze,
Snuffling around in the roots and leaves.

And looking as if it was up to mischief –
Like it might just belong to...A TRUFFLE-THIEF!
So ever so slowly, without making a sound,
Mr Snuffles poked his snout around.
To see who it was behind that tree,
Helping themselves to *his* truffles for free...

But when he peeked, there was nobody there –
The snout had *vanished*, into thin air.
And behind the tree, nestling bold as brass,
Was a *half-snuffled* truffle, left behind in the grass.
Well that was that! There was no longer doubt;
"Half-snuffled truffles and vanishing snouts!"

"And *muddy* footprints!" fumed Mr Snuffles.
"*Someone's* been helping themselves to MY truffles!"

So with no time to lose, and as fast as could be,
Off he set through the brambles and trees.
Down the winding woodland trail,
As fast as he could on the truffle-thief's tail...

And no sooner had he turned the very first corner,
Than who should he meet but his friend Mr Snorer.
(Looking dressed for a party, coming hurrying by,
And awfully smart, in a spotty bow tie.)
So with no time to lose, Mr Snuffles exclaimed,
"There's a THIEF on the run!" And began to explain:
"Yes it seems, Mr Snorer, there's a *pilfering* swine,
Who's been helping himself, to those truffles of mine.
I missed him by a whisker, just moments ago,
And helping himself to *my* truffles, you know.
It was *definitely* him, I spotted his snout –
From behind *that* tree, over there, sticking out..."

But before he could get any further than that
Mr Snorer gave his pot belly a pat
And with a gulp, and a swallow, shook his head
With bulging eyes, hiccupped, and said:

"What a – hic-up – kerfuffle! Stolen truffles?
You know that I'd help if I could, Mr. Snuffles
But I'm afraid I've got somewhere I really must be –
A dear friend's – hic-up – *surprise* birthday tea."
Then hiccupping again, he said his goodbyes
And set off to give his 'friend' the surprise
Without *even inviting* Mr Snuffles to go
(Which *might've* been nice, on *his* birthday you know!)
"Very well let him go!" huffed Mr Snuffles,
"See if I care!" and on he shuffled
Secretly wondering *who* this 'friend' might be
And a little bit jealous of their birthday tea...

In fact, he was thinking *he* wouldn't mind a surprise,
When two more friends came hurrying by.
It was Gnaw and Gnawma, the Snorey Boars,
(Looking smart, and dressed for a party what's more.)
So with no time to lose, Mr Snuffles explained,
The stolen-truffle-kerfuffle all over again:
"Yes it seems, Gnaw and Gnawma, there's a *pilfering* swine,
Who's been helping himself to those truffles of mine.
I missed him by a whisker, just moments ago,
And helping himself to *my* truffles, you know..."

"A *dear* friend's party?" Mr Snuffles muttered.
"A *surprise* birthday tea?" he angrily spluttered.
But *who* on earth could that possibly be?
And why has nobody thought about...*ME*?
"When it's *my* birthday too!" he thought with a frown,
Feeling very upset, left out and let down.
And thinking what a birthday, *this* promised to be,
Without any friends, and a truffle-less tea!
But pretending to himself that he wasn't upset,
He put on a brave face, and off he set.
Telling himself if his friends wouldn't help,
He'd catch the truffle-thief all by himself.

And no sooner had he turned the very next bend,
Than who should he meet but another dear friend.
What a stroke of luck, it was Herbert the Hoggle –
With his little wee hoglet, Herby the Sproggle
(And they looked dressed for a party *too*
Though *whose* it could be he hadn't a clue.)
So with no time to lose, Mr Snuffles explained
The stolen-truffle-kerfuffle all over again:
"Yes it seems, Herb and Herby, there's a *pilfering* swine
Who's been helping themselves to those truffles of mine.
I missed him by a whisker, just moments ago
And helping himself to *my* truffles, you know.
I've asked Mr Snorer, and the Friendly Boars too
But they aren't half as helpful, or kind as *you*..."

But before he could get any further than that
The Hoggles gave their pot bellies a pat
And with a gulp, and a swallow, shook their heads;
With bulging eyes, hiccupped, and said:

"Very sorry – hic-up – to hear that old bean
This thief sounds sneaky, and frightfully mean
We'd love to help – hic-up – but we're running late
For the *surprise* birthday bash...of a *very* good mate!"
Then hiccupping again, they said their goodbyes
And set off to give their 'friend' the surprise
Without *even inviting* Mr Snuffles along,
(The cheek! On *his* birthday!) And then they were gone.

"What!!!" gloomed Mr Snuffles, "They're going too?
Am I the *only one* who's missing this do?"
But who on earth could the party be for?
If Mr. Snorer was going, and the Friendly Boars?
And now it turned out that Herbert the Hoggle
Would also be going, with Herby the Sproggle.
"Well, with guests like *those* it'll be a wonderful tea
It's just a shame," he moped, "no one thought to ask *me*!"
Indeed what a shame, and an upsetting day,
For not only had he let the thief get away
But now it turned out *all* his friends were going
To a *surprise* party! On *his* birthday! Without *him* knowing!

For although he'd bumped into them all by chance,
No one had told him at all in advance
About this surprise party, nor *who* it was for
And he'd had *no invite*, that much was sure!
So, let down by his friends on *every* front
Not to mention the truffle-less snuffle-hunt,
He sniffled out loud it was time to head home
To a truffle-less birthday, all on his own
In a grumpy, hungry, miserable state –
And in no kind of mood to celebrate...

And as he was having these upsetting thoughts,
A familiar feeling stopped him short.
He wrinkled his snout, and waggled his tail,
There was *something* wafting down the trail:

A wafting whiff, adrift on the breeze
Whiffily wafting its way through the trees,
And the closer he got to his own front door
Whatever was wafting, whiffed all the more.

His keen little eyes began brightly twinkling
His whiskery snout began twitching and wrinkling
(*Whatever* it was, was deliciously *stinking!*)
As it whiffily wafted from under his door
And out of his kitchen windows some more,
Down the garden path, and over the gate,
His quivering nostrils could hardly wait,
And into the wood where the toadstools sprout
Until, at long last, it reached his snout!

Well! Imagine how he responded to this:
The look in his eyes was one of pure bliss.
And in a truffle-drunk and trance-like state,
With his snout he dreamily nudged open the gate,
And so wonderfully whiffy, when he sniffed, was that stink
That not even once did he stop to think
Of *why* there were truffles inside *his* house
(Truffle-snufflers, you see, aren't known for their nous.)
Indeed, why *was* his kitchen full to the brim
With truffles that hadn't been snuffled by him?

And *another* snuffler might've asked on the spot,
If there was someone inside, or not?
A truffle-thief, perhaps? Who *shouldn't* be there?
But Mr. Snuffles simply *did not care*!
And given *that* odour, the chances were slim
That such *sensible* thoughts would occur to him.
So instead as if under its hypnotic spell
Mr. Snuffles followed that wafting smell
Down the path, and towards his front door –
And swatted it open with one of his paws
And peeked his snout and tusks around
You'll never guess who, or what he found...

"SURPRISE!!! HAPPY BIRTHDAY MR. SNUFFLES!!!"
As he snuck his head around the door
It was *him* all along, the party was for,
And there in his kitchen were all of his friends
Who hadn't forgotten him in the end.
As he shook his snout slowly, in disbelief
He realised *his friends* were "the truffle-thief".
And they'd been snuffling for truffles, all day together
For *his* surprise party! "Well I never!"
And as for all of those *half-eaten* clues?
Well, they'd helped themselves to a truffle or two.

And the *wrinkly* snout, behind that tree?
It was Mr Snorer's! He'd munched two or three!
And as truffle snuffling's a hungry old biz,
He couldn't begrudge them a couple of his.
But all these here were for Mr Snuffles,
And that, my friends, was a lot of truffles.
Yes he couldn't believe his gleaming eyes,
Truffle pastries, puddings and pies
And the biggest cake he'd ever seen,
A cake beyond his truffliest dreams
Overflowing and dripping with truffles...

...Happy Birthday Mr Snuffles!

Lightning Source UK Ltd.
Milton Keynes UK
UKRC01n0251040518
322088UK00005B/18

But before he could get any further than that
The Boars gave their little pot bellies a pat
And with a gulp, and a swallow, shook their heads;
With bulging eyes, hiccupped, and said:

"Very sorry – hic-up – to hear that old fruit
Got somewhere to be, we really must shoot
We'd love to help – hic-up – but we can't you see
Got to dash to a dear friend's *surprise* birthday tea!"
Then hiccupping again, they said their goodbyes
And set off to give their friend the surprise,
Without *even suggesting* Mr Snuffles go too,
(Which *today* of all days seemed a rude thing to do!)